The use of too many  avoided, as it is more encourage comment and discussion than to expect particular answers.

Care has been taken to retain sufficient realism in the illustrations and subject matter to enable a young child to have fun identifying objects, creatures and situations.

It is wise to remember that patience and understanding are very important, and that children do not all develop evenly or at the same rate. Parents should not be anxious if children do not give correct answers to those questions that are asked. With help, they will do so in their own time.

The brief notes at the back of this book will enable interested parents to make the fullest use of these **Ladybird talkabout** books.

Publishers: Ladybird Books Ltd . Loughborough
© Ladybird Books Ltd 1974
Printed in England

compiled by Ethel Wingfield

illustrated by Harry Wingfield

The publishers wish to acknowledge the assistance of
the nursery school advisers who helped with the
preparation of this book,
especially that of Mrs. Nora Britton, Chairman,
and Miss M. Puddephat, M.Ed., Vice Chairman
of The British Association for Early Childhood
Education (formerly The Nursery School Association).

talkabout
clothes

Clothes for hot weather

Clothes for cold weather

Tell the story

today

1

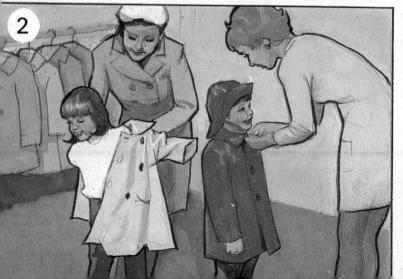

2

there will be rain . . .

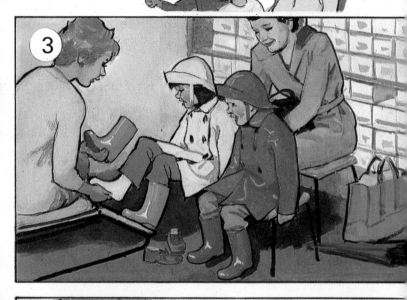

Talk about feet
and what we
wear on them

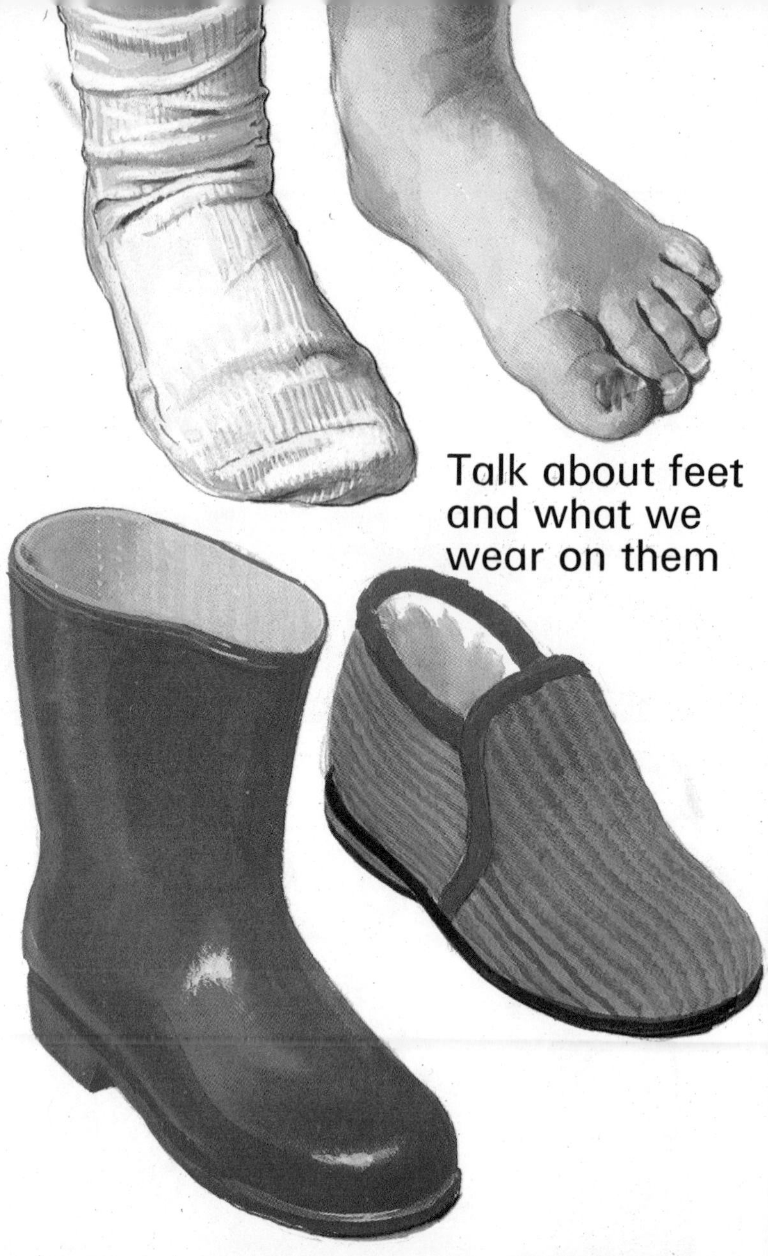

LOOK and find
another like this

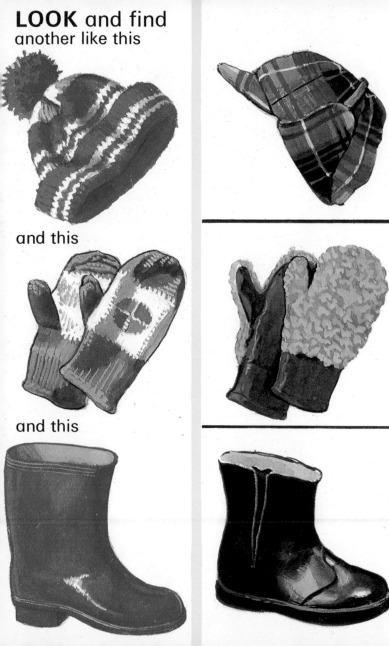

and this

and this

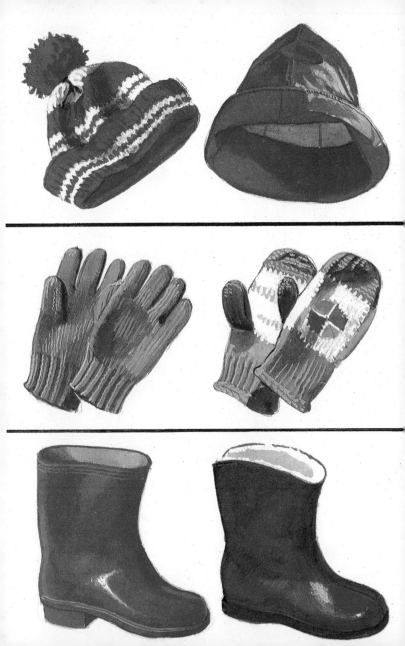

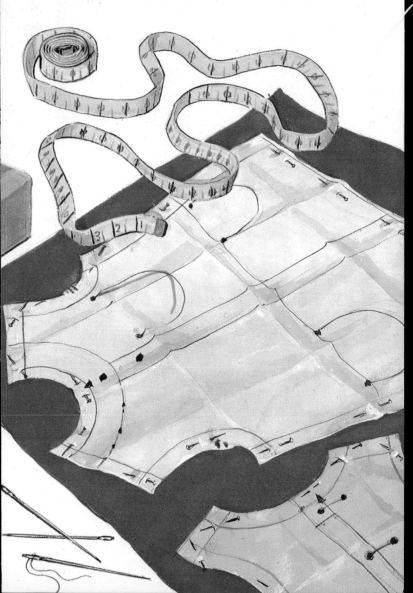

Where did each piece come from?

Talk about sewing by hand

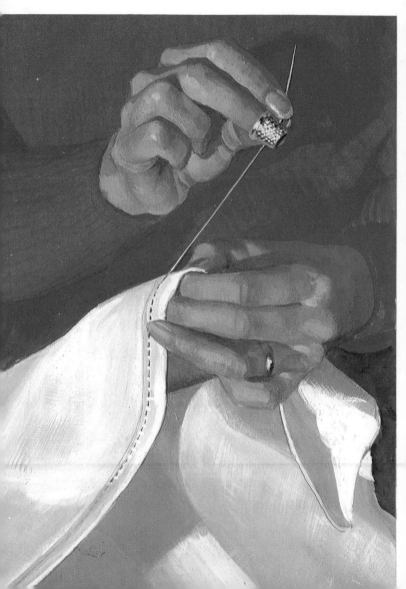

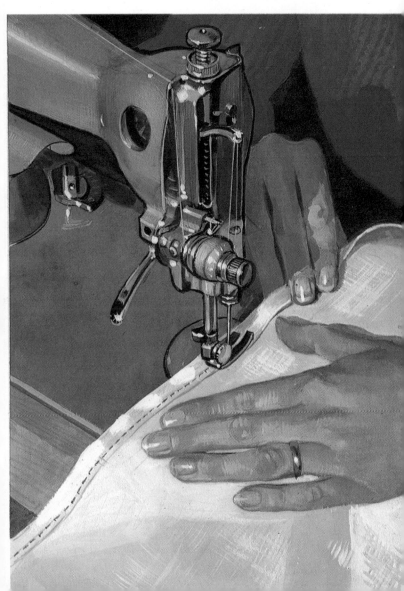

1

How to Knit a suit for Teddy

2

Talk about **left** . . .

and **right**

Talk about colours   Follow the

wool from the ball to the knitting

Where has each patch been sewn?

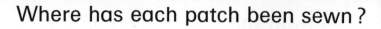

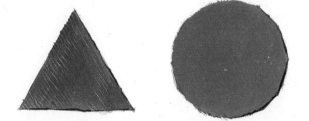

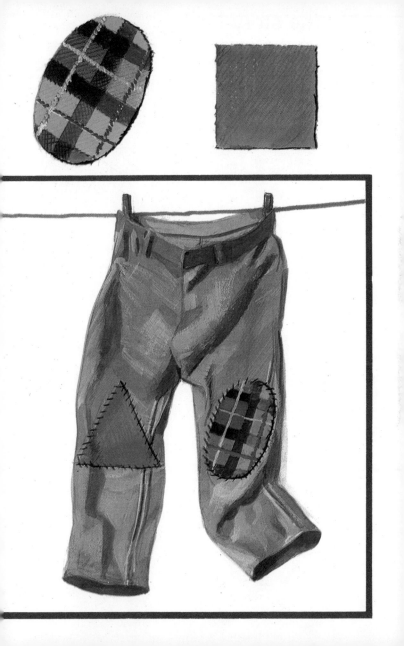

Tell the story

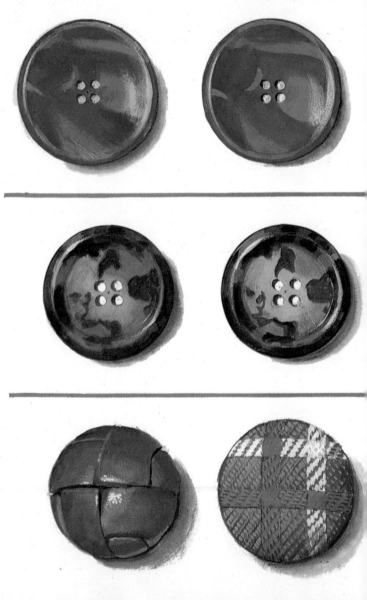

Count the buttons

1

2

3

4

5

6

Can you see
what is wrong?

Talk about keeping warm

People wear clothes

Animals have hair or wool

Birds have
feathers

1 Tell the story

Talk about what each person does

for work

Clothes for sports and games

Talk about these men

and their clothes

Talk about fastenings

Have your

Which can **you** fasten?

shoes got buckles or laces?

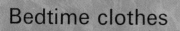

Bedtime clothes

Suggestions for extending the use of this **talkabout** book . . .

The illustrations have been planned to help increase a child's vocabulary and understanding through conversation, and the page headings are only brief suggestions as to how these illustrations may be used. For example, when looking at the 'Where has each patch been sewn?' illustrations, you can also point out which patch is **a square,** which is **a circle** and which is **a triangle.** Your child might like to find other articles around the house that are squares, circles or triangles.

When discussing the 'Look and find another like this' pages, you can talk about the feel of some of the materials, such as the softness of the woollen gloves and the smoothness of the plastic hat and Wellingtons. Let your child actually feel some wool and plastic or other materials while you talk about them. Again, on the same pages (and elsewhere), visual aids